The Hare
and
the Tortoise

2)13

13 8 '8 }

Retold by Elizabeth Adams

Illustrated by Andy Rowland

W
FRANKLIN WATTS

First published in 2009 by
Franklin Watts
338 Euston Road
London
NW1 3BH

Franklin Watts Australia
Level 17/207 Kent Street
Sydney
NSW 2000

A CIP catalogue record for this book is available
from the British Library.

ISBN 978 0 7496 8526 3 (hbk)
ISBN 978 0 7496 8532 4 (pbk)

Series Editor: Jackie Hamley
Series Advisor: Dr Hilary Minns
Series Designer: Peter Scoulding

Printed in China

Franklin Watts is a division of
Hachette Children's Books,
an Hachette Livre UK company.

This kind of story is called
a fable. It was written by
a Greek author called
Aesop over 2,500 years
ago. Fables are stories
that can teach something.
Can you work out what
the lesson in this fable
might be?

"You're so slow!"
Hare teased Tortoise
one day.

"Yes, but I bet I can beat you in a race," Tortoise laughed.

Hare agreed to
the race.

Fox chose the start
and the finish line.

start

Hare and Tortoise started the race together ...

8

9

... but Hare was so sure he would win that he lay down to sleep.

Tortoise crawled on until she got to the finish line.

Then she lay down to sleep.

15

When Hare woke up, he raced to the finish line ...

... but Tortoise was already there!

18

"Tortoise wins!" cried Fox.

Puzzle Time!

a

b

c

d

e

f

Put these pictures in the right order and tell the story!

fast

quick

slow

steady

Which words describe Tortoise
and which describe Hare?

Turn over for answers!

Notes for adults

TADPOLES are structured to provide support for newly independent readers. The stories may also be used by adults for sharing with young children.

Starting to read alone can be daunting. **TADPOLES** help by providing visual support and repeating words and phrases. These books will both develop confidence and encourage reading and rereading for pleasure.

If you are reading this book with a child, here are a few suggestions:

1. Make reading fun! Choose a time to read when you and the child are relaxed and have time to share the story.
2. Talk about the story before you start reading. Look at the cover and the blurb. What might the story be about? Why might the child like it?
3. Encourage the child to retell the story, using the jumbled picture puzzle as a starting point. Extend vocabulary with the matching words to characters puzzle.
4. Discuss the story and see if the child can relate it to their own experience, and perhaps think about the moral of the fable.
5. Give praise! Remember that small mistakes need not always be corrected.

Answers

Here is the correct order!

1. a   2. e   3. c   4. f   5. d   6. b

Words to describe Hare:
fast, quick

Words to describe Tortoise:
slow, steady